Ghost Game

Find out more spooky secrets about

Ghostville Elementary

Ghostville Elementary

Ghost Game

by Marcia Thornton Jones
and
Debbie Dadey

illustrated by Jeremy Tugeau

A
LITTLE APPLE
PAPERBACK

SCHOLASTIC INC.
New York   Toronto   London   Auckland   Sydney
Mexico City   New Delhi   Hong Kong   Buenos Aires

No part of this publication may be reproduced in whole or in part, or
stored in a retrieval system, or transmitted in any form or by
any means, electronic, mechanical, photocopying, recording,
or otherwise, without written permission of the publisher.
For information regarding permission, write to Scholastic Inc., Attention:
Permissions Department, 557 Broadway, New York, NY 10012.

ISBN 0-439-42438-0

Text copyright © 2003 by Marcia Thornton Jones and Debra S. Dadey.
Illustrations copyright © 2003 by Scholastic Inc.
SCHOLASTIC, LITTLE APPLE, and associated logos are trademarks
and/or registered trademarks of Scholastic Inc.

12 11 10 9 8 7 6 5   3/0

Printed in the U.S.A.   40
First printing, January 2003

*To Becky Dadey, Lea Johnson,
Lauren McGuinty, Alexa Fryer, and
Megan Hartley*

— DD

*To Pat and Don Cundiff — true blue
basketball fans! And to the real
Lewanna the Iguana!*

— MTJ

Contents

THE LEGEND

Sleepy Hollow Elementary School
Online Newspaper

**This Just In: Something spooky is happening
at Sleepy Hollow Elementary!**

Breaking News: Giant balls bounce out of control! Snow falls in the teachers' lounge! Weird things are happening at the after-school program. It all started right after Mr. Morton's third-grade class got moved to the basement. Could the legends be true? Is the basement haunted? And have the ghosts of Sleepy Hollow started to haunt the rest of the school? This reporter, for one, hopes not. But until we know for sure . . . whatever you do, don't stay after school!

Your friendly fifth-grade reporter,
Justin Thyme

1
Ghost Genius

"Shh," Cassidy warned her friends Nina and Jeff. "We're not supposed to be in the building before school starts."

Cassidy stared down the steps that led from the playground into the basement of Sleepy Hollow Elementary School. According to a legend as old as mud, the basement was haunted. That's how the school got the nickname Ghostville Elementary.

Cassidy didn't believe in legends. She believed in proof. She had seen the ghosts of Sleepy Hollow with her very own eyes. Her friends Jeff and Nina had seen the ghosts, too, but the rest of the school had no idea that a ghost class really did live in their classroom.

"We have to hide this basketball from

Andrew," Jeff said. "Or he'll pop it just like he did my soccer ball. He'll do anything to keep us from practicing for the after-school basketball tournament." Andrew was the class bully and the captain of one of the top teams in the play-offs. The kids were trying to sneak the ball into the building before Andrew could see it.

Nina was the best athlete in the third grade, and she was determined to beat Andrew's team in the championship game next Friday. The teams had been practicing for three weeks. Still, the thought of facing ghosts scared her silly. She tossed back her long, dark hair and nodded. "Let's make this fast and quiet. I don't want to wake up any ghosts."

Nina took a shaky breath and followed her friends down the crumbling steps. A chill tickled the back of Nina's neck as they stepped into their basement classroom. Just enough weak sunlight filtered through the grimy classroom windows so the kids could see without turning on the lights. Someone had shoved four of the oldest desks underneath the basement windows.

"Who moved our desks?" Cassidy asked, wondering if the classroom ghosts had been up to mischief again.

Cassidy's class had been moved into the basement because the rest of the school was too crowded. Up until then, no one other than the janitor had been in the basement classroom for more than 100 years. The ghosts had made it clear from the start that they did *not* want to share their room.

That's when Cassidy came up with the idea of making the room look like the ghosts' old one-room schoolhouse. There were old-fashioned desks, photos from the historical society, and even an old coal stove that Cassidy's class used to store art supplies. It was like a living museum and she thought it would keep the ghosts happy.

Cassidy and Nina forgot about ghosts

for a minute. Nina knew she shouldn't be playing in the classroom, but she couldn't resist when she saw the empty space where their desks usually stood. She popped Jeff's ball from under his elbow, dribbled it across the room, and tossed it back. Before the ball reached Jeff, it stopped in midair and then flew over to the windows.

"What's going on?" Jeff asked as the air around the ball started to glow. The glimmering slowly took the shape of a boy wearing a striped shirt and overalls. He hovered above Cassidy's desk, the oldest desk in the classroom.

"It's Ozzy," Cassidy told Jeff.

"Our ghost is back!" Nina said with a gulp.

Ozzy nodded. "Sadie and my sister, Becky, have taken a liking to that orange ball."

"Sadie?" Cassidy said.

"Becky?" Nina asked.

"Play," a girl's voice interrupted. "I

want to play orange ball." Dust clouds made of tiny green diamonds floated in the air. The dust clouds slowly turned into three more ghosts.

Becky, a girl a couple of years younger than Ozzy, hovered over one of the desks. She wore a gingham dress and had long curly hair that floated in the air above her head. Another girl with long stringy hair, Sadie, sat hunched at a desk in the corner. She looked like the saddest person in the world. A huge black-and-gray dog floated near Cassidy's desk. The dog stretched his paws up on the windowsill. The kids knew the dog's name was Huxley. They recog-

6

nized all the ghosts from an old class photo they had found in a scrapbook in the library. A poster-sized copy of the photo now hung in their classroom.

Becky danced in the air. "I want to play," she said.

"Tired," Sadie moaned. "I am so fretfully tired of sitting here wasting time away. Might we play orange ball?"

"Yip! Yip!" Huxley added.

"It's not called orange ball, it's called basketball," Jeff said.

"We know what it's called," Ozzy told him. "We played something like it right after the good Dr. Naismith invented it."

"But our ball was not as nice," Becky said. "Pa made it out of cowhide and sawdust. I like your orange ball better. It's much prettier and it bounces ever so high."

Jeff didn't have the slightest idea who Dr. Naismith was, and he didn't care. "We can't teach you to play," he said. "There's no basketball hoop in here."

"I reckon I could be the hoop," Ozzy said as he tossed the ball up in the air and caught it with his belly.

"Cool," Jeff said. "Can you teach me to do that?"

"We can't play basketball in the classroom," Cassidy interrupted. "We'll get in trouble."

"Noooooo?" Sadie asked. Slowly she faded from sight. Huxley and Becky both jumped down from the old desks. As they did, they disappeared, too.

"Aw, shucks," Ozzy said, glaring at Cassidy. He plucked the basketball from his belly and squeezed it with both of his ghost hands. *Whoosh!* The air swished out of the ball. Ozzy deflated just like the ball, disappearing as the flat ball dropped with a thud to the ground.

"Hey," Jeff yelled. "Come back here and fix my ball."

The flattened basketball zoomed up from the floor and slammed into Jeff's stomach.

Jeff sat down to catch his breath. "Nobody can play now because Ghost Genius ruined my ball."

The ball floated up from the floor. Slowly, before the kids' eyes, it inflated. Only, it didn't stop when it got to be the size of a normal basketball. Instead, it grew bigger and bigger and bigger.

"Make him stop," Nina whimpered. "It's going to blow!"

2
Ghostly Tantrum

Ozzy stopped inflating the ball just before it popped. It was two times bigger than a normal basketball. Jeff covered his head as it bounced over him in a crazy zigzagging pattern.

Cassidy ducked behind a chair. Nina hid under Mr. Morton's desk.

"Stop!" Jeff yelled. "That's my ball. Give it back!"

The three friends could no longer see the ghosts, but they knew they were there. Ghosts were like that. They only showed themselves when they wanted to.

"Nina played in the classroom," Ozzy said.

Cassidy frowned at Ozzy. "That's different," she said.

"We want to play," Ozzy cried out.

"Play," Becky groaned.

"Playyyyyy," Sadie cried.

Their three voices joined together to create a wind of noise that opened the covers of books and fluttered the pages. Pencils rolled off the tops of desks and the old map hanging over the chalkboard jiggled loose from one hook.

"They're tearing up the classroom. Do something!" Nina screamed.

"Okay!" Jeff hollered. "We'll teach you to play." The sudden silence was as loud as the ghostly tantrum. The giant ball rolled across the floor and Jeff picked it up.

"The first thing you have to learn is how to dribble," Jeff said to the air around him. "You can only use one hand at a time." Jeff dribbled the ball so the ghosts could watch him. Suddenly, the ball flew out of his control. It bounced up and down, as if by itself.

Jeff couldn't help but laugh. "It's like playing ball with the Invisible Man."

Cassidy looked puzzled. "How can you

dribble the ball?" she asked the ghosts. "Why doesn't it go right through you like everything else?"

"We concentrate," Ozzy's voice said from the corner of the room. "And some of us are a might better at it than others."

"I'm fixing to get better," Becky's voice said from behind Nina. "Just give me a bit more time."

"Time," Sadie's voice moaned from the front of the room. "We have plenty of time."

Nina bit her lip and stared at the door leading to the hallway. "You may have time, but we don't," she said.

"Nina's right," Cassidy added. "It's almost time for school to start. Mr. Morton might walk in." She knew all about getting in trouble. She had spent many recesses in detention, thanks to Ozzy's pranks.

The ghosts didn't care. They were having too much fun. They bounced the ball between them, playing keep-away from

Jeff, Nina, and Cassidy. The giant basketball bounced higher and higher until it reached the ceiling. Then it ricocheted around the room so fast it became a blur. A chair toppled over. Huxley barked and raced after the giant ball.

"Be careful," Nina yelled as she reached for the basketball.

Unfortunately, the ghosts were not in the mood to listen and the ball smashed right into the oldest desk in the room. The desk teetered. It tottered. Finally, it fell. One corner broke off in little pieces on the floor.

"No!" Cassidy cried. "That's my desk."

"My desk," Ozzy's voice echoed. "That is *my* desk."

"And that's my ball," Jeff hollered. "Give it back before you break something else."

Jeff darted after the ball, but it zoomed out of his reach and across the room. It flew toward the door just as Carla and Darla stepped inside.

Whack! The giant basketball whomped Carla dead in the stomach. She doubled over.

"You are in trouble," Darla said, bending to help her twin sister.

"Big trouble," Carla gasped.

3
Ghost Control

"If I ever see Ozzy again, I'm going to give him a piece of my mind," Jeff told Nina and Cassidy after school.

"Are you sure you have a piece to spare?" Nina said with a giggle.

Mr. Morton had banned the three friends from the after-school program for the day after Carla and Darla told him what happened in the classroom. Cassidy, Nina, and Jeff were serving their detention in the back corner of the library near the school scrapbooks.

"Very funny," Jeff told Nina. "But you won't be laughing when I outscore you in the practice game tomorrow."

"We'll see about that," Nina said.

"We're all on the same team," Cassidy

told her friends. "You should worry about beating Andrew's team in the tournament instead of each other."

"Nothing to worry about," Jeff said. "Andrew won't know what hit him when our team blows his team off the court."

Cassidy pulled a big scrapbook off the shelf. "Right now, let's find out how to control these ghosts before they ruin our lives completely."

"They've already ruined mine," Jeff complained. "Mr. Morton was so mad, he took away my brand-new ball."

"He'll give it back at the end of next week," Nina reminded him.

"The tournament will be over by then." Jeff slapped the wooden table. "I need it now so I can practice. I want to win that trophy."

"Shh." Mrs. Temple, the librarian, frowned at the kids.

"Now you know how I felt," Cassidy whispered as Mrs. Temple walked away

from her desk. "Ozzy used to pick on me all the time." Cassidy was glad the ghosts had found someone else to bother.

"It *is* sad," Nina said.

Jeff nodded. "I know. How am I supposed to practice without a ball?"

Nina shook her head. "I'm not talking about you. Those poor ghosts have been stuck in that basement for more than a hundred years."

"Maybe they like being in the basement," Cassidy said. "Maybe it's like their home."

Jeff tapped his fingers on the scrapbook and stomped his feet on the floor. He hated sitting still. "The ghosts are never happy in any of the movies I've seen," he said.

"Maybe they'd be happier if they got out of the basement once in a while," Nina said, looking up from the scrapbook.

Cassidy pushed aside the book and hopped up. "If the ghosts want out of the basement, why don't they float up the steps?"

"Ghosts can't just float anywhere," Jeff told her. "Something from the real world keeps them in a certain place."

"What would keep ghost-kids in the basement of our school?" Nina asked. She took the scrapbook from Cassidy and studied the picture from long ago. Ozzy, Becky, Sadie, Huxley, a teacher and at least ten other children were lined up in front of a small one-room school-house. "Their school was so small compared to what Sleepy Hollow is today," she said softly.

Jeff looked over Nina's shoulder. "According to this article, they rebuilt Sleepy Hollow on the foundation of the old school. They built it higher and made it bigger."

"Maybe the ghosts don't know that there is a whole new school above their heads," Cassidy pointed out.

"I bet that's why they never left the basement," Nina said.

"It's a good thing," Cassidy said. "At least we're safe from the ghosts when we're upstairs."

"In the movies I've seen, people are never completely safe," Jeff warned.

Just then, the kids heard a bloodcurdling scream, and it wasn't coming from the basement.

Cassidy looked at Nina and Jeff. "Uh-oh!" she said. "Jeff may be right!"

4
Ms. Finkle

The kids followed the screams down the upstairs hallway to the basement door. Ms. Finkle, their principal, stood staring down the steps. Her hair stuck up straight and she was as stiff as a statue.

Cassidy waved her hand in front of Ms. Finkle's face, but their principal didn't flinch. "She's frozen," Cassidy said.

"Cool," Jeff said. "Can we keep her that way?"

"Do you think she saw a ghost?" Nina whispered, ignoring Jeff.

Cassidy shrugged. There was no telling what Ozzy or one of the other ghosts might have done. This ghost thing was getting way out of hand. Ms. Finkle might be the principal, but she wasn't mean. Ozzy had no right to scare her silly.

Ms. Finkle reached her hand up in the air and pointed down the steps. "It . . . it went that way," she managed to say.

"Don't worry," Cassidy said quickly. "We'll find the problem." The three kids took off down the steps, leaving Ms. Finkle staring into space.

"We have to tell Ozzy to stop bothering us," Nina said, gathering up her courage.

"While you're at it, you can tell him to bake us cookies and do our homework," Jeff said with a smirk. "He's never going to stop haunting us just because we tell him to."

"Very funny," Cassidy said as the kids jogged down the steps. "But we have to do something. We can't let the ghosts scare people whenever they feel like it."

"Ghosts don't do what people ask," Jeff pointed out. Suddenly, he lunged off the steps and grabbed a huge lizardlike creature.

"Oh, my gosh!" Cassidy squealed. "What is that?"

"This," Jeff said, cupping the creature in his hands, "is a baby iguana."

Nina leaned away from the baby iguana. She did not like animals with scales and beady eyes. "It's almost as disgusting as a hairy spider," she said.

Everyone in their class knew Nina was deathly afraid of spiders.

"That must have been what scared Ms. Finkle," Cassidy said with a nervous giggle. "It wasn't Ozzy after all."

"It's just one of Olivia's pets," Cassidy called up to Ms. Finkle. "We'll handle it." Olivia was the school's janitor and was known for taking care of stray animals.

"Let's go find her and give her this . . . thing," Nina said.

"Couldn't we keep it to scare Ms. Finkle?" Jeff asked.

"No way!" Cassidy said, pointing him down the dark hallway.

Nina kept far away from the snapping iguana and called for the janitor. "Olivia! Olivia?"

The only sound was a tapping from behind a closed door. "She must be in here," Jeff said.

"Wait a minute," Nina yelled. "Don't open that door!"

But it was too late. Jeff had already gone inside.

5
Trapped

"It's all right," Jeff said, pulling a light cord. "It's just a janitor's closet."

The two girls followed Jeff inside the room. "Is Olivia in here?" Cassidy asked.

"Olivia?" Nina called again.

The only answer was the slam of the door. Cassidy grabbed the doorknob, but it wouldn't budge. "We're trapped!" she said with a gulp.

Nina looked at the iguana squirming in Jeff's hand. "It's worse than that. We're trapped with an iguana monster," Nina said. She reached for a broom in case the lizard got loose, but the broom was too fast for Nina. It danced out of her grasp and boogied around the closet. A mop and bucket joined the broom, zigzagging between Nina, Cassidy, and Jeff.

"What's happening?" Nina squealed.

"I want to play orange ball," a voice chanted.

"It's Becky," Cassidy said. She ducked as a bucket sailed over her head.

"WE WANT TO PLAY! WE WANT TO PLAY!" voices chanted from all around the kids.

"She's not alone," Nina yelled. She dodged a dancing mop and desperately tried to pull open the door.

"I can't play!" Jeff yelled at the bouncing broom. "Because of you, my ball was taken away!"

An unseen hand tossed a bucket of water in Jeff's face. "Bleck!" Jeff screamed and wiped at the water with his free hand. "I wouldn't play with you if you were the last ghost on earth!"

The mops didn't stop dancing. The buckets didn't stop flying and the brooms didn't stop bouncing. They chased the kids around and around until Nina, Cassidy, and Jeff were trapped in a corner.

27

"WE WANT TO PLAY! WE WANT TO PLAY!" the ghosts chanted over and over.

Nina put her hands over her ears to drown out the noise, but she couldn't take it anymore. "All right!" she screamed. "You can play!"

The brooms, mops, and buckets fell to the ground and for a moment there was silence. Then one tiny voice asked, "When?"

Nina took a deep breath and said, "Soon."

Slowly, the door swung open and before anyone could say boo, the kids and the iguana raced out of the closet and smack-dab into Carla and Darla.

6
A Promise

The ghosts were quiet all the next day, but Nina still had trouble keeping her mind on work. If she wasn't looking for Olivia's iguana, she was being bothered by Andrew.

When Andrew swiped her favorite eraser, she ignored him. When he threw paper wads in her hair, she batted them away. But when Andrew tossed a plastic spider on her desk, she jumped up and screamed.

Mr. Morton looked up from the piles of papers he was grading. "Is there a problem?" he asked.

Nina sputtered. She stammered. She took a deep breath. She knew if she told on Andrew he would never leave her alone.

"I . . . I . . . I saw a spider," she said, feeling her face growing red. She heard Andrew snicker. "It's gone now," she added.

And it was. That's because Jeff had reached over and swatted the toy spider to the floor.

As soon as Nina sat down Cassidy patted her on the arm.

"I hate spiders," Nina said. "And I hate lizards and turtles and Olivia's iguana."

"Lewanna is back in her terrarium," Cassidy whispered. "Olivia said she would keep the iguana tucked safely away in her office. You don't have to worry."

"I hope you're right," Nina whispered back.

"Now," Jeff said, "if we could just lock up Andrew with the iguana, we'd be okay."

Nina glanced at Andrew. He grinned and held up another rubber spider. This one had giant hairy legs. "Too bad you missed yesterday's practice," he hissed. "My team was hotter than ever. You don't stand a chance next Friday!"

Nina tried not to pay attention to him, but Andrew was one of those kids who was hard to ignore. "We're number one. We're number one," he kept whispering whenever Mr. Morton wasn't watching.

Carla and Darla glared at them. "Shh," Carla warned.

"Or you'll get in trouble . . ." Darla added.

"Again," they both said at the same time.

Carla and Darla would know. When they told Olivia the kids had been playing in the storage closet, Olivia was not happy. As soon as Lewanna the iguana was tucked safely in her terrarium, Olivia made Cassidy, Nina, and Jeff clean up the mops and buckets and brooms. Thanks to Carla and Darla, the three kids had been late getting home.

As soon as Carla and Darla turned back to their work, Cassidy stuck out her tongue at them.

When the day was finally over, Nina, Cassidy, and Jeff waited for the rest of the class to file out the door before packing up their stuff. They wanted to be as far away from Andrew as possible. They didn't have to worry about Carla and Darla because they were always first in line.

As Nina tried to pass through the door, she felt like a wall of ice blocked her way. Cold air made the hair on her arms stand straight up. Nina jumped back and knocked into Jeff.

"What is wrong with you?" he asked.

"Something is here," Nina said, rubbing the goose bumps from her arms.

Cassidy felt the cold, too. It seemed to go right through her. "We have company," she said. "Ghost company."

Ozzy's voice wrapped around them. "Remember what you told us," he said.

"You told us we could play orange ball," Becky's voice said.

"Today," Sadie added.

Nina nodded. "I remember," she said.

Cassidy sighed. "You'll have to wait until after our practice game against Andrew," she said. "Then we'll come back for you."

"Promise?" Becky asked.

"Promise," Nina said.

Jeff pulled Nina and Cassidy beside the water fountain as soon as they left the room. "I can't believe you made a promise to a ghost!" he told Nina. "Don't you know a ghost never forgets a promise?"

"How would I know that?" Nina asked.

"It's in just about every ghost movie ever made," he told her.

"I don't waste my time watching old movies," Nina argued.

"None of us has time to waste," Cassidy interrupted. "And that's just what we're doing. Wasting time while Andrew and his team are practicing in the gym."

Jeff took a deep breath. "Cassidy is right. What's done is done. Let's get to the gym before the after-school program is over."

Andrew's team was already practicing. Nina hated to admit it, but they looked good. Andrew dribbled the ball between his legs and then threw it crosscourt to a teammate. When he got the ball back, he jumped for the basket. The ball sailed through the net.

Andrew grinned at Nina, Jeff, and Cassidy. "I got the moves," Andrew said, "to guarantee you lose!"

"What a show-off," Jeff said. "We can do better than that. Let's show him!"

The game started and Andrew stole the ball right from Nina's hands. "You snooze, you lose," he said. "Again!" The next time she got her hands on the ball, he stepped in front of her and forced her into a charging foul.

"Loser," Andrew teased.

Later, when Nina tried to get the ball from him, she accidentally hit his arm. Another foul. Of course, Andrew made the free throws and his team won the practice game. Andrew pumped his fist in the air and chanted, "We're number one. We're number one!"

"What was wrong with you today?" Jeff asked Nina after practice as they headed for the gym doors.

"You weren't on top of your game," Cassidy added. "Let's go to my house.

You'll feel better after a little TV and a snack."

"We can't go to your house," Nina said. "I have to be home for dinner in two hours and we still have to go back to the basement."

"Are you crazy?" Cassidy asked.

"Crazy or not," Nina answered, "we have a game to play . . . with the ghosts!"

7
Ghost Experiment

"A promise is a promise," Nina told her friends, pulling them back downstairs to their classroom. "We told them we would play with them and we have to keep our word," she said.

Nina opened the door to their classroom. She didn't see anyone, but she knew the ghosts were there. "Okay, let's go upstairs and play basketball."

Immediately, green glowing shapes surrounded the kids. They gradually turned into Ozzy, Becky, Sadie, and Huxley. More ghost haze hovered near Nina, but she waved it away with her hand.

"We are to stay in the cellar," Sadie said. "We cannot leave."

"It will be okay," Nina said. "We'll show you the way."

"I want to go upstairs and play orange ball," Becky said with a stomp of her foot. Her foot went through the floor and disappeared for a minute.

Huxley barked.

"You forgot to think hard about making your foot solid," Ozzy told his sister.

"I know, I know," Becky said. "I can do it." She closed her eyes and thought hard. It worked. Her foot became solid. Unfortunately, it was still stuck in the floorboards. When she tried to take a step, Becky stumbled to her knees and Huxley jumped up to lick her face.

"Let me help you," Ozzy said. But Becky shook her head. "I can do it all by myself!" And she did, though it was obvious that Becky had to work harder at making things solid than Ozzy did.

Once Becky was free from the floor, she put her hands on her hips. "I am ready to play," she said as if nothing strange had happened. "Now!"

Ozzy thought about it for a full

thirteen sec-
onds. Finally,
he nodded. "Let's go!"
Ozzy, Sadie, and Huxley
jumped from their desks and
floated over the floor. Becky didn't
just float; she danced. Nobody noticed
one more shadow following the group.

Cassidy held open the door and waited
for the ghosts to float into the hall. The

40

farther they got from the room, the dimmer their shapes became. By the time they reached the stairs, the three ghost-kids and their dog were barely more than a fog. "I'm feeling a might poorly," Ozzy said, his eyes wide with fear. "I feel weak."

"They're disappearing!" Nina squealed.

"Don't let me float away," Becky cried and grabbed at Nina with almost invisible hands. "It's getting darker. I can't see. Help me!"

Nina had never seen anyone look so afraid, but she didn't know how to help.

Sadie hovered just above the floor. "Can't go any moooore," she wailed. "So sad. So, sooooo sad."

"Make it stop!" Becky screamed.

Cassidy could barely see Huxley. He had disappeared almost completely and his howl sounded very distant, as if he were in a deep well.

"They're losing their strength," Jeff said.

"Think," Nina told Jeff. "Didn't one of those old movies you're always watching tell how to stop this?"

Jeff shook his head. "Nothing like this ever happened in the movies I've seen. Never!"

"I know what it is!" Cassidy said with a snap of her fingers. "When we first found out about Ozzy, you told us that sometimes ghosts get power from something they owned."

Jeff nodded. "That's right." He thought about it for a moment. "Maybe they can't go upstairs unless something from their time goes with them."

"But we don't have anything that belonged to them," Nina said.

"Yes, we do," Cassidy said. "We have their desks."

"Those desks are really heavy," Jeff said, looking up the tall steps. "We'd never get them upstairs."

"I know!" Cassidy said, jumping up and down. "We could take the piece that broke off my desk."

"Do you think that will be enough?" Jeff asked.

Nina nodded. "It's worth a try," she said.

"Becky, Ozzy, Sadie, and Huxley might not be here when we get back," Cassidy said. "We have to help them get back to their room."

"I know just what to do," Jeff said. "Wait here." He rushed back into the classroom and came back out with three big pieces of cardboard. He handed one each to Cassidy and Nina. "Follow me," he said.

Jeff got behind the ghosts and then he started waving the cardboard in the air. Nina and Cassidy joined him. They fanned and fanned until the faint haze that was the ghost-kids slowly started moving back toward the room. The closer they got to the door, the stronger they became. Finally, the last ghost was through the door. With their gathered strength, they floated toward the old-fashioned desks in the center of the room.

Huxley panted beside Ozzy. Their forms were still dim, but now the kids could see the ghosts' faces again. They seemed very, very pale. "Thank you," Sadie said. "Thank you kindly."

"But we didn't get to play," Becky said, her lower lip stuck out. "And they promised."

"I told you," Jeff muttered to Nina. "A ghost never forgets a promise."

44

"Don't worry," Nina said. "We have a plan. You wait here."

The kids crept along the hallway, past cold drafts and cobwebs. Finally, they reached Olivia's office. Cassidy slowly opened the door.

"CAW!"

Cassidy jumped back and knocked into Nina. Nina bumped into Jeff. All three landed on the floor.

"Is it another ghost?" Nina asked, her voice trembling.

Cassidy peeked back into the room and shook her head. "No, it's another one of Olivia's pets — a black bird." The three kids untangled themselves and stepped into the room. The bird was perched in a big cage. Next to the furnace was an empty aquarium. A turtle looked at them from the middle of the floor.

Jeff rummaged through a big trash can. "Got it!" he said as he held up a hunk of wood from Cassidy's desk.

"Hurry," Nina said as Jeff ran back across the room. "We shouldn't be in here." Jeff, Cassidy, and Nina turned to leave, but a huge shape blocked the door.

Olivia stood in the doorway. Lewanna was perched on her shoulder. As soon as the iguana saw the kids, it hid its head inside one of Olivia's red overall pockets. Olivia gently stroked its back. "Never fear, Lewanna dear," Olivia said.

Olivia's earrings jingled. Or maybe they jangled. "What, may I ask, would three third graders be doing with an old piece of wood?" she asked.

Jeff thought up a fib and he thought it up fast. "It's for a science experiment."

"That's right," Cassidy added. "We need to test objects to see what floats and what sinks." Nina nodded and inched toward the door.

"Just remember this," Olivia said as the kids squeezed past her. "Sometimes experiments fail. Consider yourselves warned!"

8
Bored Ghosts

"The coast is clear," Jeff said, flinging open the basement door. Huxley whined from the bottom of the steps. "No," Becky wailed. "We'll fade away again."

Nina patted Becky on the shoulder. "Don't worry," Nina said. "Everything will be all right this time."

Becky smiled at Nina as Ozzy yelled, "Let's go!"

The ghosts tumbled right over Jeff, grabbing the wood from his hand. He was pretty sure someone went through him, too. "Give me that wood!" Jeff snapped, shivering from the cold blast.

The ghosts were too excited to listen. They zoomed up the steps in a whirlwind of green haze and flew into the hallway in every direction. Green shadows were everywhere.

"OOOH!" Ozzy exclaimed. "What happened to the fields?"

Becky squeezed beside Ozzy. "I don't like this place," she said. "It's scary."

Nina couldn't believe anyone would like the dark basement better than the bright modern hallway.

"What is that?" Sadie asked, pointing to a digital clock hanging near the ceiling.

Nina started to answer when Huxley barked. The kids found him floating around in the computer room. Green light glowed from the screens.

"Saints preserve us!" Ozzy yelped and flew back across the hall. "This must be magic."

Cassidy giggled. "Not magic. Technology." Cassidy was a whiz at computers and she was glad to explain everything to the ghosts.

Sadie's eyes grew wider and wider as

Cassidy told how the kids used the computers to find information and write reports. "All that with a press of a button," Cassidy said, showing them how to turn on the machines.

"Oh!" Sadie gasped. "Whatever else can you do?"

"Televisions are the best thing," Jeff said before Cassidy could talk more about computers. "There are movies and sports games."

"Television?" Ozzy asked.

Jeff turned on the television in the corner of the room and a cartoon blared. "Wow!" Ozzy said, staring in fascination. "How did those funny little people get in the box?"

"How did they get so tiny?" Becky asked.

"They're not really tiny," Cassidy said as she switched channels.

"Perhaps they are ghosts as well," Sadie suggested.

Jeff laughed and started to explain

when a rock band came onto the screen. Loud music filled the computer room.

Ozzy wailed. Becky screeched. Sadie cried. Huxley howled. Another ghostly cry sent shivers up Nina's neck.

"It's terrible," Sadie added, covering her ears. "Sooooo terrible."

Before Nina, Cassidy, or Jeff could explain, the ghosts flew across the room and surrounded the television. They rocked it back and forth.

"It's okay," Cassidy told the ghosts. "It's just music."

"Stop!" Jeff yelled. "You're going to break it."

"Do something," Nina said. "They don't understand."

Before the kids could tell them about modern music, the ghosts disappeared without a trace.

"I wish I'd never gotten the idea to help the ghosts," Nina said. "We have to find them before they break something or someone sees them."

Cassidy gave Nina a quick hug. "Don't worry, we'll find them," Cassidy said.

At that moment the kids heard a piercing scream. "I think we're too late," Jeff said. The kids raced down the hallway toward the scream.

They found Ms. Finkle sprawled on the office floor. White papers flew all around her while the copy machine spat out more copies. "That machine is crazy!" she screamed.

Jeff pulled the plug just as the kids heard a big crash from the nurse's office. The nurse ran screaming from her office. She pointed back to her room. "There's something in there," she yelled.

Cassidy, Jeff, and Nina rushed into the nurse's room at the same time a huge wad of bandages flew into the air.

"Yikes!" Nina screamed. "It's the attack of the killer bandages."

Jeff knocked bandages off his arms. "No," he said seriously. "It's the attack of the bored ghosts. They've been locked up for more than a hundred years and now they're finally free. The same thing happened in *Runaway Ghost*. They never did catch the ghost in that movie."

"But we have to stop them and get them back downstairs where they belong," Cassidy said.

Jeff nodded. "The only way to do that is to get that piece of wood from your desk."

A loud popping noise sent the kids scrambling for the cafeteria. White fluffy popcorn exploded onto the cafeteria floor and the ketchup pump squirted all by itself. "Stop it!" Nina screeched to the invisible ghosts. "You're messing up our school!"

Ozzy's laughter filled the cafeteria. "It's our school now!" he yelled.

Jeff swirled around, trying to catch a glimpse of a green ghost shadow, but he saw nothing. "If we could just see them, maybe we could catch them," he muttered.

Cassidy ran into the kitchen and came back out with a huge bag of flour.

"This is no time to bake a cake," Jeff told Cassidy.

Cassidy rolled her eyes at Jeff and pulled out a handful of flour. "This will help us see them. Watch this!"

Cassidy tossed flour all over the cafeteria. Soon white powder covered every surface of the room, but the ghosts were still nowhere to be seen. "Where did they go?" Nina asked.

"I guess it didn't work," Cassidy said.

"Wait," Nina said. "Look, there's Ozzy!" The kids stared at a flour-covered Ozzy. He smiled at them and said, "BOO!" The flour flew off him and hit the kids like a dust storm.

"He's gone," Jeff said. It was true — the cafeteria was completely deserted.

Cassidy's face was as pale as the flour. "How in the world are we going to catch them now?"

9
Ghost Deal

Flour settled on Cassidy's eyelashes and tickled her nose. She stomped her foot, sending a white powdery cloud all the way to her knees. "Catching invisible ghosts is impossible!"

"I'll tell you what's impossible," Olivia said from the doorway. "Kids making messes."

Nina gulped as Olivia made her way across the littered floor of the cafeteria. With every step she took, the buckles on her red overalls clinked. Or maybe they clanked. Either way, it was loud. Olivia towered over the kids like Godzilla eyeing an afternoon snack.

"I'll make you *all* a deal," Olivia said. "I'll keep this mess a secret as long as you get it cleaned up in fifteen minutes."

The kids had no choice. They made the deal. Nina sighed as soon as Olivia left. "Now that the ghosts can get out of the basement, we'll end up cleaning up after their hauntings morning, noon, and night."

Jeff kicked at the flour on the floor. "This is rotten," he sputtered. "The ghosts are the ones that should be making deals. Not us."

Nina thumped Jeff on the shoulder, sending a cloud of flour floating over his head. "That's it!" she said. "We need to make another deal — a deal with the ghosts."

"What kind of deal?" Jeff asked. "The deal to take them upstairs didn't work out very well."

"You'll see," said Nina.

"Whatever it is, we'll have to find them first," Cassidy said.

"And we'll have to find them fast," Nina said, "or our parents will start worrying about us."

Just then, a scream echoed down the

hall. "That shouldn't be too hard," Jeff said. "All we have to do is follow the screams."

The kids forgot about Olivia's deal and raced down the hallway. They ended up in front of the teachers' lounge. "I must find the janitor," Mr. Morton yelled as he rushed from the room. He held a coffee mug in his hand and his glasses were fogged up. "This is an emergency!"

Mr. Morton hurried down the hall and Cassidy put her hand on the doorknob.

"We can't go in the teachers' lounge," Nina said. "It's anti-kid territory."

"It's anti-ghost territory, too, but that didn't stop them," Cassidy said, pulling the door open.

The air was so cold that a fine frost layered the windows and the kids could see their breath. Coffee had turned to black muddy ice in the teachers' coffeemaker. "The teachers will be grouchy tomorrow without their coffee," Jeff said. "This is a disaster."

Cassidy spied a small piece of wood sitting on the windowsill. She knew what it was as soon as she saw it — the piece of her desk. "They're here," she said. "The ghosts are in here." She dived for the wood, but Ozzy was too quick. The wood floated in the air high above the kids.

"This is it. You have to go back downstairs now," Cassidy said. A cloud of cold air formed with every word she spoke.

"No," Becky said. The kids looked up as she slowly took shape. She was hanging from a light fixture. "We don't want to go back to the basement."

"Noooo," Sadie moaned. "There is nothing to do down there."

"We're having too much fun," Ozzy said. He appeared right behind Nina and tickled her ribs. Nina shivered and jumped away.

"Yip. Yip," Huxley barked and became visible.

Cassidy took a deep breath. "If you

don't go back to the basement," she said in a voice that meant business, "we will never play with you again."

"Never?" Sadie asked. "Ever?"

"Never," Jeff said, catching on to Cassidy's plan.

The ghosts were silent for a few minutes, except for Huxley, who was busy scratching an ear.

"We don't care," Ozzy said. "Now that we know how, we'll have fun playing with all the things in this new school. We don't need you."

Nina looked at the clock in the teachers' lounge. They only had a few minutes before Olivia would be there. Nina was desperate. "We'll make you a deal," she said.

"Deal?" Ozzy asked. "What kind of deal?"

"We'll play you in a game of basketball. If we win, you have to stay in the basement. If you win, you can go wherever you want," Nina said.

"Orange ball?" Becky asked. "I like orange ball."

"You mean if we win, we can go upstairs anytime we like?" Ozzy asked.

"And we won't bother you," Nina said with a nod.

Cassidy had a sinking feeling.

Becky danced around the room and sang. "We're going to win. We're going to win!"

In fact, Becky sang so loud the kids didn't hear the door open, but they did hear the screams.

10
Play Ball

"What are they doing here?" Jeff asked.

The twins, Carla and Darla, had taken one look at the floating ghosts in the teachers' lounge and fainted.

Cassidy kneeled on the floor and patted Carla on the face, while Nina and Jeff tried to get Darla to wake up. "Are you okay?" Nina asked Darla.

Darla rubbed her eyes. "We were looking for Mr. Morton to ask him a question," she said. "But I thought I saw . . ."

". . . a ghost," Carla finished.

"Don't be silly," Cassidy said. She hoped the ghosts were well hidden. "You must have seen a shadow."

Carla slowly nodded. "Of course . . ."

". . . there are no such things as ghosts," Darla said.

"But what are you doing here . . ." Carla began.

". . . in the teachers' lounge?" Darla finished.

"We're working on a project," Nina explained. She wasn't *really* lying. Getting the ghosts back to the basement was a huge project.

Nina helped up Carla. Jeff helped Darla. "You'd better hurry," Jeff said, "or you'll get in trouble for being in the teachers' lounge." Everyone knew that Carla and Darla never got in trouble. Ever. They were out the door before Jeff could say another word.

Cassidy sighed. "A face-off with the ghosts?"

"We have no choice," Nina told her. "Besides, I'm the best player at Sleepy Hollow. Those ghosts don't have a chance."

"You're not any better than me," Jeff said.

"But we'll beat all of you," Ozzy said, reappearing next to Jeff.

Cassidy stepped between Ozzy and Jeff. "There's no time to argue. Let's go play ball!"

The gym was deserted, except for Andrew. He was practicing his free-throw shot. "So that's how he gets so good," Cassidy said.

"We have to get rid of him," Jeff said.

"Maybe he could help us win," Nina suggested.

"No way," Jeff said. "I'd rather be haunted for the rest of my life."

"You may get your wish," Nina said, pointing to Ozzy. He had tiptoed up behind Andrew and tapped him on the shoulder. When Andrew turned around, Ozzy became invisible, flew around him, and stole his ball. Becky and Huxley joined Ozzy in a game of keep-away with Andrew's ball. Andrew had no idea what was going on. The ghosts laughed at Andrew before disappearing. The ball bounced around the gym, all by itself.

"I'm getting out of here!" Andrew

screamed. He grabbed his bouncing ball and ran out of the gym.

Jeff couldn't help laughing. "Way to go Ozzy! You showed that show-off!"

Becky hopped around the gym. "Let us play now. Let us play now!"

Nina got a ball from the storage closet and showed it to the ghosts. "The point of the game is to throw the ball in that hoop and to stop the other team from scoring. Your team gets two points every time you make a basket. We'll play to twelve."

Ozzy grabbed the ball. "I know what to do," he said.

"In our game we used fruit baskets hung from trees," Sadie told them in her sad voice.

"Dr. Naismith said the game should be played with a soccer ball," Ozzy added. "We didn't have one of those so we had to use Pa's homemade leather ball."

"We couldn't bounce the ball or run with it. We threw it back and forth,"

Becky said. "This orange ball will be much more fun."

Ozzy slowly bounced the ball, concentrating so his hand didn't slip right through it. Nina couldn't stand it. She had to steal that ball.

With one quick motion, Nina lunged toward the ball. Ozzy was fast. He swerved around and the ball went through his chest. Ozzy bounced it on the other side of his body.

"No fair!" Nina yelled. "You can't pass the ball through your body."

Ozzy grinned. "You can if you're a ghost."

Sadie nodded. "Play," she said, slapping her hands together. "Let me play."

Ozzy tossed her the ball, but he threw it too hard. The ball zipped right through Sadie's stomach and bounced off the concrete gym wall.

"Now that's what I call a pass," Jeff said with a laugh.

Nina grabbed the ball and raced down

the court. She threw a perfect shot, but Ozzy was quick. He flew up and caught the ball in midair.

"No fair!" Nina squealed. "You can't fly in basketball."

Jeff laughed. "I don't remember seeing any rules that say you can't."

"Ha-ha," Nina said. "You're so funny I forgot to laugh."

Ozzy passed the ball to Becky. Becky had trouble dribbling. The ball kept going through her hand. Ozzy finally grabbed it from her and tossed it to Sadie.

Sadie drifted over Cassidy's head and perched above the hoop. She calmly re-arranged her tattered dress around her knees before dropping the ball through the net.

"Two points," Ozzy said, cheering for his friend.

Just then, a green haze swirled in the center of the court. It grew until it was the size of a boy. The haze turned smoky,

becoming thicker and more solid until a
very tall boy stood before them.

"Meet Nate," Ozzy said.

There, standing a head taller than
everyone else, was a barefoot ghost boy.
His jeans were six inches too short and
dirt smudged his chin. He crossed his
eyes and stuck out his tongue at the kids.

Nina shrieked. Cassidy gasped. Jeff gulped. The ghosts laughed. Nate never said a word. He just floated around the gym. It gave Nina the creeps.

Nina and Cassidy stared at each other while Jeff grabbed the ball. The ghosts were ahead. "We've got to beat them," Cassidy whispered to Nina. "If we don't, Sleepy Hollow Elementary School is doomed!"

11
Ghost Team

"*Swish!*" Nina sang as her basketball zoomed through the net.

Cassidy was so happy she jumped up and down. "We're tied."

"Lucky shot," Ozzy said as he dribbled past. The ball touched the floor but Ozzy's feet didn't.

Becky danced around Nina. "You have to get more points than us, not the same amount."

"She's right," Jeff said as he grabbed the ball away from Ozzy and tossed it toward the basket.

Jeff missed the easy layup, but Cassidy cheered for him anyway. "You'll make it next time," she yelled. Jeff hoped he would. This wasn't like playing in the tournament; this game *really* mattered. It was the game of a lifetime. Jeff had to get the ball back. It would be just like in the movies, where he would sink the winning shot and be a hero.

"*Swish!*" Nina made a basket. Nina was good, but Ozzy matched her shot for shot. Soon, the score was ten to ten and the ghosts had the ball.

Nate swooped up to the ceiling and dive-bombed toward the hoop.

Nina screamed, "He's going to make it!"

The ghosts were sure they were about to win the game.

"We're doomed," Cassidy moaned.

"Not if I can help it," Nina said. She jumped as high as she could, but it wasn't high enough. She couldn't reach Nate.

"Quick, step into my hands," Jeff told Nina. Nina stepped into Jeff's cupped hands and he lifted her as high as he could. It was high enough. Nina swatted the ball away before Nate could dunk it.

Cassidy caught the rebound and passed it to Jeff. Jeff threw it to Nina as

she made her way back down the court. Before Ozzy could stop her, Nina shot the ball. Cassidy held her breath as the ball rolled around on the rim.

Nate flew toward the ball, but he was too late. It dropped through the net with Nate flying through after it. A loud wail filled the gym as the ghosts realized they had lost.

Ozzy did not like losing. He dived for the ball, plucked it from the gym floor, and then blew air into the ball so fast the kids barely had time to duck before it exploded into a million pieces.

"You did it!" Cassidy yelled to Nina as pieces of basketball floated through the air. "You beat the ghosts."

Nina looked at Jeff. "No," she said, "we all beat the ghosts. We did it as a team."

"How did you ever think of giving me a boost?" Nina asked Jeff.

Jeff shrugged. "I saw it in a movie once."

Ozzy slowly flew over to Cassidy and handed her the ghost wood. "A promise is a promise," he said.

Jeff wiped sweat from his brow and hoped that the ghosts would be true to their word.

"At least you got plenty of basketball practice for the tournament," Cassidy told her friends.

Jeff sank to the floor beside Cassidy. Somehow, winning the tournament didn't seem so important anymore. They had saved the school and that was enough — at least for today.

Ready for more spooky fun?
Then take a sneak peek at the next

Ghostville Elementary

#3 New Ghoul in School

Jeff sighed. Studying the presidents was as exciting as watching his toenails grow.

"Who can tell me the name of the president of the United States?" Mr. Morton asked.

The new kid raised his hand high over his head.

Mr. Morton wiped chalk dust from his

glasses and peered around the classroom. Edgar was the only one with his hand up. "Edgar?" Mr. Morton said.

Edgar straightened the heavy wire-rimmed glasses on his nose and sat up straight in his chair. "The president of the United States is Grover Cleveland, sir," he said with a grin that showed a big gap between his two front teeth.

Carla and Darla gasped. A few kids giggled. Andrew laughed out loud.

"What's wrong with the new boy?" Nina whispered to Cassidy and Jeff.

"Cleveland was president more than a century ago," Cassidy said. She knew all the presidents because she had spent an entire afternoon looking them up on the Internet for a report.

Jeff shrugged and looked around their classroom for something more interesting than presidents to think about.

He felt as if he was in the middle of a history book. Their classroom was decorated to look like the inside of a one-room schoolhouse from the 1800s. There were antique desks and even a coal-burning stove they used to store art supplies. Pictures of kids from more than a century ago hung on the walls. Sometimes Jeff pretended they were scenes from scary movies. His favorite painting showed a boy with heavy wire-rimmed glasses sitting all by himself under a tree reading. Jeff imagined the limbs coming to life and slowly encircling the boy and his book.

He looked at the painting while Mr. Morton talked on and on about presidents. Jeff frowned. Something was wrong with the scene. The tree was the same, but . . . the boy was gone. The boy had disappeared from the painting!

About the Authors

Marcia Thornton Jones and Debbie Dadey got into the *spirit* of writing when they worked together at the same school in Lexington, Kentucky. Since then, Debbie has *haunted* several states. She currently *haunts* Ft. Collins, CO, with her three children, two dogs, and husband. Marcia remains in Lexington, KY, where she lives with her husband and two cats. Debbie and Marcia have fun with spooky stories. They have scared themselves silly with *The Adventures of the Bailey School Kids* and *The Bailey City Monsters* series.

Creepy, weird, wacky, and funny things happen to the Bailey School Kids!™ Collect and read them all!

The Adventures of

THE BAILEY SCHOOL KIDS